Message
from Africa

Penn Mullin

High Noon Books
Novato, California

Cover Design and Interior Illustrations: Nancy Peach

International Standard Book Number: 1-57128-059-6

9 8 7 6 5 4 3 2 1 0
2 1 0 9 8 7 6 5 4 3

You'll enjoy all the High Noon Books. Write for
a free full list of titles.

Contents

Corina and Zack are young co-workers at the Park Museum. They are assistants to the museum's director, Claire Long, who sends them to the "four corners of the world" on exciting explorations.

CHAPTER 1

A Message from Africa

"You wanted to see us?" Corina and Zack walked into the office of their boss, Claire.

"Yes! Are your passports up to date?" the pretty gray-haired woman asked with a smile.

"I think so!" said Corina. "Do you have a trip for us?" Her eyes flashed with excitement.

"How about Zimbabwe (Zim-BOB-way) in Africa?" Claire asked. "There's big news over there. I just saw it on the Internet. You've heard of the famous walled city of Great Zimbabwe?"

"The one where all the people vanished?" Zack asked. "And no one knows where they went?"

"Yes. The experts think they may have found where these 'lost' people went!" Claire said. "It's deep in the forest near the Zambezi River. Are you interested?"

"Yes!" said Corina and Zack together.

"Great! I thought you might be," Claire laughed. "I'd like to go myself. But this sounds like it could be quite a rough trip. Better you than me! You two are used to those things."

CHAPTER 2

The Road to Great Zimbabwe

"Corina and Zack? From the Park Museum? Welcome to Zimbabwe!"

"Thank you! And you are Zhanta (ZON-ta)?" Corina and Zack shook hands with the tall handsome African who stood smiling at the airport gate.

"Did you have a good trip?" he asked as he picked up their bags.

"A *long* trip!" said Zack, stretching out his arms. "Someday they will make airplane seats

3

for people with long legs!"

"I can't believe we're really in Africa!" said Corina. "I've always dreamed of this."

"I'm glad your museum sent you," Zhanta said. "This is going to be a great trip. Two people from our museum here in Harare (ha-RARR) will go with us to the lost village. Come, my truck is just outside."

Corina and Zack followed Zhanta out to the front of the airport. The halls were filled with people in brightly-colored African dress as well as business suits.

Soon they were driving through the wide tree-lined streets of Harare, the capital of Zimbabwe.

"It's hard to believe we're in Africa," Zack said. "Tall buildings, traffic, crowds."

"Harare has really grown from when it was the small city of Salisbury (SALZ-burry). That was its name when we were still a British colony," Zhanta explained. "And this country was still called Rhodesia (Ro-DEE-sjah). When we became an independent country in 1980, the name was changed to Zimbabwe."

"What does that name mean in your language?" Corina asked.

"In our Shona language it means 'Houses of Stone,'" Zhanta said. "And that is where I am taking you first – to see the largest of all stone houses: Great Zimbabwe. The city that was abandoned back in 1450."

"How far away is it?" Zack asked.

"Only a few hours after we are out of the city," said Zhanta.

"How about wild animals? Will we get to see any as we drive?" Corina asked.

"Maybe a few zebras or giraffes. But not many. Once great herds of animals freely roamed these plains," Zhanta said. "But big tobacco and corn farms have taken over. Most of the animals are now in the national parks. We will pass through Hwange (Ha-WANG-eh), our largest park. That's where the biggest elephant herds are."

Now all around them the grasslands

stretched out wide and green. Gentle sloping hills led up to rocky ledges.

"I feel as big as an ant out here!" Corina said. "The land seems to go on forever!"

"Zimbabwe is almost as big as your state of California!" Zhanta reminded them.

"And Zimbabwe looks so small on the whole map of Africa!" Zack said. "Africa is *huge*!"

"Tell us more about Great Zimbabwe, Zhanta," Corina asked. "I can't wait to see it. And find out more about why the Shonas suddenly left their city."

"There are other mysteries at Great Zimbabwe, too," Zhanta said. "The Shonas had no written history. There were only stories, handed down over the years. We do know that the city was built between the years 1000 and 1450. It became a huge center of power in southern Africa. With 10,000 to 18,000 people!"

"That's a lot larger than I thought!" Zack said.

"And Great Zimbabwe was rich! There was a lot of copper and gold mined here. Traders came from Arabia, Portugal, even Asia!" Zhanta said. "Pieces of dishes from China have been found in the ruins!"

"Think of how *long* it took to get here from China back then!" Corina said.

"Yes, people came from China. But British

explorers did not reach Zimbabwe until the 1850's!" said Zhanta.

"Didn't one of them find Victoria Falls?" asked Zack.

"Yes, Dr. David Livingstone. He was searching for the beginning of the Zambezi (Zam-BEE-zi) River," Zhanta said. "Then he suddenly came to those huge falls. A mile and a half wide and 350 feet high! He was the first white man ever to see them. He named them after the Queen of England – Victoria, in 1855."

"They're the largest falls in the world, aren't they?" asked Corina.

"Yes. You'll get a great view of them when we cross the Zambezi River," Zhanta said.

"That's supposed to be such a wild river," Corina stared at Zhanta.

"We will be on a good strong footbridge. It is not too bad." Zhanta smiled. "You just do not look down!"

CHAPTER 3

A City of Stone

"We are here – Great Zimbabwe!" Zhanta stopped the car at the top of a hill above the ruins.

The old stone city sat in a valley below a wooded hillside. Its rock walls were curved into a large circle. Parts of other walls were scattered all along the valley floor. Some reached up onto the rocky hillside.

"This was quite a city!" whispered Corina as she looked down on Great Zimbabwe. "It's kind of ghostly. It's hard to believe 18,000 people once lived here and then just disappeared

"Let's go down for a closer look," Zhanta said. They left the car next to several others in a parking lot. Then they began to walk towards the high wall. On their way they passed many other smaller stone walls shaped in circles.

"Some of these walls were built around markets. Others made huts for people and corrals for cattle," Zhanta explained.

They walked on until they came to the largest stone wall of all.

"It's a lot higher up close!" Zack said.

*"Some of these walls were built around markets.
Others made huts for people and corrals for cattle."*

"Thirty six feet high and 820 feet around!" Zhanta said. "This is called the Great Enclosure. It took almost a million blocks of granite to build!"

"Where did they get all the rock?" asked Corina.

"From the hills around here," Zhanta said. "And look at this." He touched some of the stones in the wall. "There is no mortar used to hold these together. The stones were all fit together by hand!"

"Think how long that took!" Zack whistled.

"Look at this." Zhanta was pointing up to a large green stone bird on top of the wall. "This was the sacred bird of the people here. It was carved out of soapstone. Seven others like it have fallen off the walls. They are now in our museum."

"It's beautiful," said Corina. "We have some small pieces of old Shona sculpture in our museum. We would love to have more!"

They walked inside the huge stone walls.

"Here's another wall! Where does this passage between them lead?" Zack asked.

"To the strange Conical Tower," Zhanta said. "Follow me."

They walked down a long narrow path with the high walls on either side.

"Tell us about this tower," Corina said to Zhanta.

"Well, no one knows what it was for. I wish my ancestors had written things down!"

"Is 'Zhanta' an old Shona name?" Zack asked their guide.

"Yes, I am named for a Shona chief who lived in the 1890's," Zhanta said.

"It's a wonderful name," Zack told him.

They kept walking down the long passage. At last the huge Conical Tower was in front of them. It was about 16 feet across at the base. It grew narrower as it got higher. At the top it was only about 6 feet across.

"Look how well these stones all fit together," Zack said. "It's a work of art. But what was it for? A prison? Storing crops?"

"There is no inside! It's solid blocks of stone!" Zhanta explained. "And there is nothing underneath it. We know it was important because of its size. Some people think it was made to look like a place to store grain. This would be a symbol of good crops and success. But only the first Shonas of Great Zimbabwe know the real secret."

The wind whistled softly in the trees beside the tower. They could hear the voices of other people coming towards them now. "Come, I will show you the ruins up on the hillside," Zhanta told Corina and Zack. They walked on back to the entrance.

"Up on the hill I will show you a Shona

rubbish heap," Zhanta laughed. "Even though they did not write things down, we can still learn about them by looking at their garbage!"

They followed their guide up the path. He stopped near a large shallow pit.

"Here we are! The garbage dump!" Zhanta stepped down into the weeds and small stones. "Come on! I'm watching out for snakes. Don't worry," he laughed. "This is where we found lots of cattle bones. So we think that was the main food for the Shonas besides their crops."

"Is this where the pieces of china were found?" Corina asked. She knelt down to look more closely at the ground.

"Yes, and beads, too. Traders brought them

here from all over Africa," Zhanta said.

Suddenly Corina gasped. "I think I found something!" She dug into the dirt. "Yes!" She held up a small bright blue glass bead.

"Way to go, Corina!" Zack said.

Zhanta looked closely at the bead in Corina's hand. "This glass bead was probably made in Egypt or Arabia. Then a trader brought it here – probably 500 years ago! It was buried in this pit until you found it today!"

"Well, this bead must go to your museum, Zhanta. It doesn't belong to me," Corina said. "I'll always remember the thrill of finding it here! Come on, Zack, your turn now!" she laughed. "Dig around in there!"

CHAPTER 4

Storm Ahead

They stood at the top of the hill and looked down at Great Zimbabwe below them.

"You've really given us the grand tour so far, Zhanta," Zack said. "Are we lucky!"

"There's so much more to show you. But it's getting late. We'll come back tomorrow and get an early start," Zhanta said. "Our hotel is close by here. Ready to start down?"

"There's a feeling of great mystery here," Corina said softly. "Why did the people suddenly leave? The ruins give us no clues."

"No, you are right. Perhaps one day we will find the answer. Some people think that the Shonas left because they had used up the land. They had farmed it to death. Mines were empty. No more grass for the cattle," Zhanta said. "But maybe we will never know. It will stay the Shonas' secret."

"I hope the village you found turns out to be where the Shonas ended up," Zack said. "Maybe there will be more clues there."

"I hope so. I wish we could find a soapstone bird or some other Shona carvings at the village. Then we could be more sure that we had found their new home," Zhanta said. "I am

21

eager to show you the village. When we get to the truck I will phone my museum friends who will meet us at the river."

"I'm a little worried about crossing that river!" Corina told him. "I have trouble with high places!"

"You will do fine! I do not worry about you!" laughed Zhanta.

They made their way down the rocky hillside in among the old stone walls.

"Have you got your blue bead in a safe place?" Zack asked Corina.

"It's zipped up tight in my fanny pack," she said. "No way am I losing this! I will deliver it to the museum myself!"

Soon they were back in Zhanta's truck. He called his friends on his cellular phone. But his face took on a worried look as he spoke.

"Hmmm. O.K. We'll get there tomorrow then. Meet you at our usual place." Zhanta hung up and said, "Tafara sounded worried. We will need to leave for the river first thing tomorrow! There is a bad storm due in 3 days. We need to be across the river before it hits!"

"A storm? We *have* to get across the river before it comes!" Corina said.

"Well, we'd better turn in early tonight then," said Zack. "Whose turn is it to type up today's notes on the laptop, Corina?"

CHAPTER 5

Danger on the Road!

"Elephants! Look! They're all over the road up there!" said Zack.

"Well, this is Hwange Park!" laughed Zhanta. "We can expect road delays." He pulled his truck to the side of the road and stopped. "The road belongs to them right now!"

"Look at that huge one with the big tusks!" said Corina. "He doesn't look friendly!"

"This is his herd of cows and calves. He wants us to know it!" Zhanta smiled.

*Suddenly the bull moved away from the
tight group of elephants. His ears flared out. He
started towards the truck. The closer he got,
the bigger he looked.*

25

Suddenly the bull moved away from the tight group of elephants. His ears flared out. He started towards the truck! The closer he got, the bigger he looked.

"Will he charge us?" Zack stared at the oncoming bull ahead in the dust.

"I don't think so. He's just showing us his power. Warning us. But I could be wrong. Hold on. I may start this truck in a hurry!" Zhanta said.

The bull was coming faster now, making a loud trumpeting sound.

Corina grabbed her door handle. Her heart was pounding. Closer and closer came the bull. Would he ram the truck and push it over?

Zhanta's foot was ready at the gas pedal.

The bull was thirty feet away now. Twenty. Thundering towards them. Zhanta, start the truck! thought Corina. She just stared, frozen, as the bull came on.

Suddenly he stopped! Fifteen feet away! He flared his ears and shook his huge head. Was he getting ready to charge?

"Don't move, anybody," Zhanta said softly. "I think he'll leave soon now."

Slowly the bull turned and started back to his herd.

"Wow! That was close," said Zack.

"This fellow came closer than I thought he would." Sweat poured down Zhanta's face.

They watched as the bull led his herd off towards a watering hole. Zhanta started up the truck. He pointed to a group of giraffes running across the plains ahead. "Aren't they beautiful? This is my favorite park of all."

"Isn't this park bigger than our whole state of Connecticut?" Zack asked.

"Yes, and we still run out of food for the elephants here. They strip the forests bare. Then the herds begin to starve. Man has taken over so much of the land that once belonged to these wild animals. It is sad," Zhanta sighed. "Well, we must keep moving. We still have quite a long way to go yet. And we *must* beat this storm to the river!"

CHAPTER 6

Over the Zambezi!

"Listen! What do you hear?" Zhanta put down the truck windows.

"A roar! Is it the river?" Zack asked.

"Victoria Falls! Look – you can see the spray already and we're six miles away!" Zhanta pointed to the fine mist that was coming down through the trees all around them.

"Those falls must be amazing – listen to that roar," Corina said. "Will we cross the river very near them?"

"Not too far below them," Zhanta said. "You might get a little wet in the mist!"

"We're in the rain forest now, aren't we?" Zack asked.

"Yes, it is all around the falls and the lost village where we are going," Zhanta said.

They drove on toward Victoria Falls. The jungle was dark and thick beside them.

"The Zambezi is really an important river for our country," Zhanta said. "It forms our border with Zambia (ZAM-bi-a). It also gives us most of our electricity."

Now spray covered their truck like rain. Suddenly there was an opening in the trees and all whiteness in front of them. Zhanta pulled into a large flat area and parked. The roar of the falls was deafening. "We're here!" he yelled. "Pull on your raingear!"

The air was thick with mist. The ground shook under their feet. Zhanta led the way to a railing ahead in the whiteness.

Suddenly the mist cleared. Now they could see the falls spread out before them!

"Ohhh!" Corina and Zack said together. Before them waterfalls stretched a mile and a half wide! Small islands were spaces in between the falls. The water crashed down into the gorge far below. Spray rose 1500 feet in the air. It seemed to touch the clouds.

"There. The mist cleared for you," said

Zhanta. "We call these '*mosi-oa tunya*' (mosee-oha-TUN-ya), the smoke that thunders."

"They are *so* beautiful!" Corina shouted to Zhanta. She began to video the falls right through the soaking spray.

Soon Zhanta was leading them back to the truck. "We must go meet the others below the falls. I am still worried about the storm."

Now they drove on through the jungle. The river was deep in its gorge beside them. Soon they pulled into a parking area beside the river.

"They are here!" Zhanta said as he pulled the truck to a stop. "We'll leave the camera and laptop in the truck."

Zhanta's museum friends rushed over.

"Tafara! (Ta-FAR-a)!" Zhanta hugged the small woman who had a bright, friendly smile. "Her name means 'we are happy' in Shona," he told Corina and Zack. Then he shook hands with the tall young man beside her. "Hi, Moyo! Meet my American friends, Corina and Zack!"

Soon they were all putting on rain jackets and backpacks. "I don't like those black clouds building up. We must go now!" Zhanta told the group.

The trail led to the edge of the deep gorge, which was filled with mist. They could hear the thunder of the river somewhere far below. And there was the start of the footbridge. It was made of steel, held up by legs that went down into the white mist of the gorge. Wide enough for only one person!

I can't see the other side! thought Corina. It looks as if you just walk out into nothingness! I don't think I can do this.

"How far is it across?" she asked Zhanta.

"Not far. Only about 300 feet," he told her. "The bridge is strong. Do not worry."

"I'll be right behind you," Zack said.

"Keep looking straight ahead," said Tafara. "That is the important thing."

If I want to see the lost village I've got to do this, Corina told herself. Claire, did you know what you were getting us into?

Zhanta led the way. Then Tafara, Corina,

and Zack. Moyo went last. Corina watched Zhanta's body quickly disappear into the mist. Then Tafara's. Now it was her turn. She stepped onto the wet metal walkway and grabbed hold tight to the railing. Everything was mist. She could see nothing else.

"I'm right behind you!" said Zack.

Corina walked slowly along. Now she was sure the bridge was swaying. She kept grabbing the railing. She could see no one – just mist.

Suddenly the mist cleared. And Corina could see where she was. She looked down. And down and down. She felt dizzy, sick. She sank to her knees.

*Suddenly the mist cleared. Corina could see where
she was. She looked down. And down and down.
She felt dizzy, sick.*

CHAPTER 7

Terror at the Gorge!

"Corina!" cried Zack. He bent over her as she sat huddled on the bridge. "It's O.K.! You'll be fine. Just rest now. Don't move."

Tafara, Moyo, and Zhanta were there now, too. "Just take your time. You're almost across!" Tafara told Corina.

"I can't do it," Corina whispered.

"Sure you can," said Zack. "I'm going to be right with you. You can see the other side now. Do not look down. Just straight ahead."

"I can't." Corina just sat there with her head between her knees.

Suddenly they heard the sound of thunder coming closer. That meant lightning, too. And they were all on a metal bridge.

"Corina," Zack said. "We have to get off the bridge. There is lightning. You have to get up and keep going. You're almost there."

Corina heard him. She knew she had to get up. She just couldn't make her body move. Then she felt Zack's arm around her shoulder, pulling her up. And she was standing.

"Just keep your eyes on me," Tafara said.

Thunder rumbled, closer now. They knew they had to get off the bridge – fast!

Corina just kept going, step by step. She watched the back of Tafara's rainjacket. And she could see the other side coming closer. Her eyes kept wanting to look down.

Suddenly lightning lit up the sky! Corina told herself, "Faster. Just go. Straight ahead. Follow Tafara."

Zhanta yelled. He was on the other side! Corina could see how close it was now. Twenty feet. Fifteen. Another flash of lightning. Ten. There! She stepped off onto the other side. Safe. Now Zack was pulling her towards the shelter of the jungle as the rain began to pound down. Thunder exploded above them.

CHAPTER 8

A Village in the Forest

The rain forest was thick and dark and damp as they pushed their way among the huge trees and vines. The air was filled with the cries of monkeys and birds high in the treetops.

"We are almost there," Zhanta said. They had been walking for two hours since leaving the river. The storm had moved on quickly.

"How did you ever find this village?" Zack asked. "It's so deep in the forest."

"Airplane. We were flying over this area,"

Tafara said. "The trees were not so thick. We were low enough to see some stone walls. And a tower!"

"Right away we got excited," Moyo said. "Maybe this was where the Shonas had gone!"

Now the forest was not so dark as before. The trees did not make such a thick canopy over their heads. Sunlight streamed down.

Zhanta stopped and set down his pack. "We are here!" he announced, smiling.

Corina and Zack stared around them. A village *here*? they were both thinking.

Tafara said, "Come. We will show you." She and Moyo led them a short ways into the forest where there was even more sunlight.

"Look at this!" she pointed proudly ahead.

There stood a stone wall in the shape of a circle. It was made of large gray stones. It was about shoulder-high on Tafara.

"Amazing! It's just like those at Great Zimbabwe!" said Zack. "You must have been flying low to have spotted this!"

"Zhanta likes to brush the tops of the trees," laughed Moyo.

"This *has* to be the Shona village!" said Corina. She walked over and touched the wall. Where did they get the stones?" she asked.

"There are rocky hills nearby," Tafara said. "You cannot see them because of the forest. We think they found gold there, too."

"And there are many streams here," said Moyo. "A good place for a village."

"We have found cow bones and farm tools just like the ones at Great Zimbabwe," Tafara said. "We are having them checked at the museum to find out how old they are. We think they were made in the 1400's. That's when the Shonas were starting their new village here."

"Look, now I can see the walls all around us!" said Corina.

"Oh, would I love to find one of those Shona carved birds in here!" said Zack.

"You'll have plenty of time," Zhanta laughed as he came up to them. "We'll be here for a few days. The museum wants us to bring back more tools to check for dates."

"Well, Corina, do you think Claire will give us a raise if we find a Shona bird here?" Zack chuckled.

"I promise – if you find a Shona bird here – we will lend a whole collection of Shona sculpture to your museum," laughed Zhanta.

"I think I'll put that offer in writing on my laptop and make Zhanta sign it," said Corina. "But I want him to agree that if we find a Shona bird he will be the one to bring the collection to America! Agreed, Zhanta?"

"Oh, he agrees," said Moyo and Tafara together. "And he will surely need two helpers to go along, right, Zhanta?"